To my stepmother Jacqui,
my niece Danielle,
and Happy Birthday, Buster.

Bon Voyage, Donna
With many thanks to Nancy, Cecilia, and Amy,
to my agent, Andrea,
and my muse, L3.

Copyright © 2000 by Woodleigh Marx Hubbard.
All rights reserved. This book, or parts thereof, may not be reproduced in any form
without permission in writing from the publisher, G. P. Putnam's Sons,
a division of Penguin Putnam Books for Young Readers,
345 Hudson Street, New York, NY 10014.
G. P. Putnam's Sons, Reg. U.S. Pat. & Tm. Off.
Published simultaneously in Canada. Printed in Hong Kong by South China Printing Co. (1988) Ltd.
Text set in Whimsy ICG and BirdlegsMdSG

Library of Congress Cataloging-in-Publication Data
Hubbard, Woodleigh. All that you are / Woodleigh Marx Hubbard. p. cm.
Summary: Celebrates the reader for following dreams, walking with confidence, standing
with courage, living with compassion, forgiving, and embracing peace.
1. Conduct of life Juvenile literature.   [1. Conduct of life.]
I. Title. BF637.C5H83   2000   158—dc21   99-21658   CIP
ISBN 0-399-23364-4
1 3 5 7 9 10 8 6 4 2
First Impression

Woodleigh Marx Hubbard

All That You Are

G. P. Putnam's Sons • New York

Today is a day
to celebrate you
because

You follow
your Dreams

You walk with Confidence

You stand with
Courage

You are
Generous

You live
with
Compassion

You are a
Loyal friend

You embrace Peace

You give Joy